This edition published by Parragon Books Ltd in 2015

Parragon Books Ltd
Chartist House
15-17 Trim Street
Bath BA1 1HA, UK
www.parragon.com

ISBN 978-1-4748-0502-5

Printed in China

Disney PRINCESS

Cinderella

Adapted by Della Cohen

Parragon
Bath · New York · Cologne · Melbourne · Delhi
Hong Kong · Shenzhen · Singapore · Amsterdam

Long ago in a faraway land, poor Cinderella lived with her mean stepfamily. They filled her days with cooking, scrubbing, washing and chores of every kind.

Cinderella's stepmother and two stepsisters, Anastasia and Drizella, never helped with her work. But Cinderella remained cheerful and kind.

She made friends with all the animals that she met.

Cinderella even made clothes for the mice who shared her small attic room.

One day, Jaq, her favourite mouse, was upset. "What's all the fuss about?" Cinderella asked. Jaq led her to a new mouse, caught in a trap!

Cinderella quickly freed the frightened mouse. Then she dressed him in new clothes and found the perfect name for him: Gus.

When it was time for Cinderella to feed the
chickens, the mice headed for the farmyard.
Cinderella always saved some corn for them.

But today, the mean old cat, Lucifer, blocked
their way. Jaq was chosen to get the cat to chase
him. Then the other mice could scoot outside.

The plan worked. Jaq kicked the cat and angry Lucifer began chasing him.

But Jaq was too fast for Lucifer and made it safely into a mousehole. While Lucifer waited for Jaq to come out, the other mice scampered by him!

derella spent the rest of her day attending
ores.

ke that ironing," Drizella demanded.

n't forget the mending," Anastasia added.

k up the laundry and get on with your

," her stepmother ordered.

Meanwhile, at the royal palace, the King
complained to the Grand Duke. "It's high time my
son got married," he sobbed. "I want grandchildren!"

The King decided to hold a ball. "If all the eligible maidens come," said the King, "the Prince is bound to find his bride among them."

Later that day, Cinderella heard a knock on the door. "Open in the name of the King," said the royal messenger. He handed Cinderella an invitation.

When her stepmother read the invitation aloud, Drizella and Anastasia became excited. Each imagined the Prince falling in love with her.

Cinderella was also excited. "Why, that means I can go, too!" she said. The stepsisters laughed.

"Every eligible maiden is supposed to attend," answered Cinderella.

Surprisingly, her stepmother agreed. "I don't see why you can't go . . . if you get all your work done, and if you can find something suitable to wear."

Cinderella raced to her room and found a dress that had
belonged to her mother. With a little stitching, she could
make it pretty.

As Cinderella worked on the dress, her stepmother and
stepsisters called for her and gave her many chores. "Get them
done quickly," said her stepmother.

When Cinderella had to put the dress aside,
her animal friends began to work on it. They
gathered beads and a sash that the stepsisters
had thrown away.

Soon they had created a beautiful gown!

Cinderella finally finished her chores and went to her room. Then she realized it was too late to get ready for the ball.

She was so sad!

Suddenly, the mice yelled, "Surprise!" They showed Cinderella the beautiful gown. "Oh, thank you so much!" she cried.

Cinderella put on the gown and hurried to join her stepfamily. But when her jealous stepsisters recognized their old sash and beads, they tore Cinderella's gown to shreds!

Cinderella's friends watched sadly as she wept in the garden. "It's no use," she sobbed. "Nothing will help."

At that moment, bright, sparkling lights began floating and swirling around Cinderella.

Poof! Cinderella's Fairy Godmother appeared. "Dry those tears," she told Cinderella. "You can't go to the ball looking like that."

"But I'm not going," said Cinderella.

"Of course you are," replied the Fairy Godmother.

She waved her magic wand over a pumpkin, and a regal coach appeared!

"Oh, it's beautiful," said Cinderella. The Fairy Godmother waved her wand again.

Jaq and Gus and two other mice turned into four beautiful white horses. Then she changed Major the horse into the coach driver and Bruno the dog into the footman.

Next, the Fairy Godmother turned Cinderella's torn dress into a beautiful gown. In a flash, there were also tiny glass slippers for her feet.

"On the stroke of midnight, the spell will be broken," the Fairy Godmother warned. "Everything will be as before."

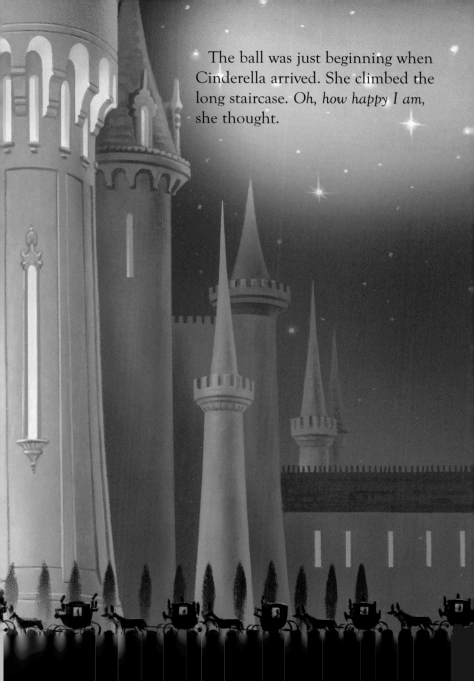

The ball was just beginning when
Cinderella arrived. She climbed the
long staircase. *Oh, how happy I am,*
she thought.

The King and the Grand Duke watched
as the maidens walked forward to meet the
Prince.

The Prince was unimpressed with them all.
Then he noticed Cinderella.

Entranced, he walked past all of the other maidens and led Cinderella into the ballroom. They began to dance.

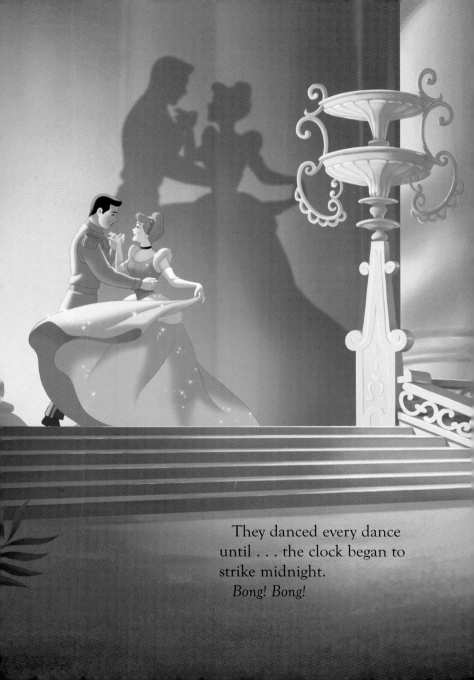

They danced every dance
until . . . the clock began to
strike midnight.
Bong! Bong!

"I must go!" Cinderella cried in a panic, freeing her hand from the Prince's.

As she fled, she lost a glass slipper on the staircase. The clock sounded as the coach raced from the palace. It was midnight!

The horses were mice again.
Cinderella was in rags. But she still had
one glass slipper.

The next morning, the Prince proclaimed that he would marry the girl who had lost her slipper at the ball.

The King was furious that the girl had vanished and demanded that the Grand Duke check every house in the kingdom for the maiden whose foot fitted the glass slipper.

The next morning, Lady Tremaine
told her daughters that the Grand Duke
was searching for the girl who lost the glass
slipper. Whoever fit the slipper perfectly
would marry the Prince!

Then, the wicked stepmother realized that it must have been Cinderella who was the Prince's favourite at the ball!

She locked Cinderella in her room.

"Let me out!"
Cinderella cried.
  But her stepmother put the
key in her pocket, laughing her
meanest laugh.
  Then Cinderella heard a knock
at the front door. The Grand Duke
had arrived!

Meanwhile, Jaq and Gus had seen what the stepmother did. They took the key out of her pocket and slipped it under Cinderella's door.

Downstairs, the Grand Duke watched his footman try to squeeze Anastasia's big foot into the slipper.

Of course, the slipper did not fit Drizella, either.

As she hurried down the steps, Cinderella heard the Grand Duke ask, "Are there any other maidens in the house?"

"Please wait!" called Cinderella. "May I try on the slipper?"

The angry stepmother tripped the footman as he approached Cinderella. The glass slipper shattered.

"Oh, no!" moaned the Grand Duke.

"But you see," said Cinderella, reaching into her pocket, "I have the other slipper." Quickly, the Grand Duke put the slipper on Cinderella's foot.

It fitted perfectly! Cinderella was the Prince's love!

Cinderella married the Prince
and lived happily ever after.

And so did Jaq, Gus and all of
Cinderella's animal friends!